# Stella and Little Tree

## Marilyn Cole

## Illustrated by Angela M. Karam

*A little Christmas story for Stella, who makes me smile.*
*~Marilyn Cole*

# Stella and the Little Tree

Marilyn Cole
*Illustrated by Angela M. Karam*

There once was a little
tree that lived on a hill by
the side of the road.

This little tree was very different from the other tall, bushy trees. For some reason, the little tree did not grow very tall or full.

Every year the little tree on the hill by the side of the road wished he could be like the other trees.

He wished the hardest during the time of the year when the days grew shorter and the air was colder.

Every year, families would
come in their cars with boxes
of bright balls and ribbons.

They would choose one special tree and adorn
it with pretty, shiny red and green decorations.

But year after year, no one chose the little tree on the hill by the side of the road.

This made the little tree feel very sad.

It was that time of the year again and many of
the trees were already decorated from top to
bottom. The little tree on the hill by the side of the
road was hoping this would be his year to be
chosen.

The sun moved lower in the sky and most of the families had left for the day, when a big car parked on the side of the road. A young family spilled happily out of the doors. The boy and girl ran towards all the large, bushy trees, trying to find the best tree.

Then a little girl peeked around from behind her father and saw the little tree on the hill by the side of the road.

The little girl named Stella started toddling toward the little tree clapping and smiling. At that same instant, the little tree felt a warmth in his trunk.

Stella had
a smile on her
face from ear to ear,
and the little tree
thought her eyes seemed
to dance. Stella made the little tree feel happy.

But the little tree still believed that the bigger
brother and sister would choose another tree.

Then a strange thing happened.

The whole family ran over to Stella and said, "Stella has found our tree!" The family began hanging all the beautiful ornaments on the little tree.

Finally Stella's mom said, "All our little tree needs is a star." Stella's dad lifted her up and she put the star on top of the little tree on the hill by the side of the road.

Then they all cheered, but none louder than Stella.

The little tree on the hill by
the side of the road was a little sad
when he saw Stella and her family drive
away, but it was indeed the happiest day of his life.

That night as the air grew colder and the stars twinkled overhead, the little tree on the hill by the side of the road was illuminated in all his splendor by the moonlight.

Just as the little tree was getting sleepy, he thought about Stella. After he had been passed over year after year, the amazing little girl with the wide smile and dancing eyes made the little tree feel special.

So on that cold, clear night, the little tree on
the hill by the side of the road felt happy and proud.

Made in the USA
Lexington, KY
03 December 2012